\+ -

DIVINE LAWS

VS

WESTERN NEGATIVE INFLUENCE

A unique, educative and thought-provoking book

By

Shannon Sheese Keys

Published by New Generation Publishing in 2018

First Edition

www.newgeneration-publishing.com

New Generation Publishing

UNLESS OTHERWISE INDICATED SCRIPTURE QUOTATIONS ARE FROM THE KING JAMES VERSION (KJV)

Table of Contents

IN THE BEGINNING

God created this world to function according to a fixed pattern called the Universal Laws of Nature. Without dark you cannot recognize light. There must be contrast. You cannot clap one hand. There is evil as well as good and there is pleasure and pain. The more science discovered these laws the more sure we are that someone planned every detail of the universe, made it and keeps it functioning according to His plan. That someone is God, the all powerful and the Ruler of the Universe. The Holy Book of the Bible tells us that our first earthly parents, Adam and Eve sinned against God and consequently the effects befall them heavily. It follows that what goes around comes around. In other words, as a man sow, so he reap. In fact, every word and thoughts have effects upon us for good or bad and for this reason purity of thoughts and words is of great importance because you are what your thoughts are. Thoughts are not physical. They are part of your psychical you. Your soul-self. The more you train your ability to think, the more you develop your spiritual strength. This is a necessity if you intend to control your future both mentally and in terms of material things.

In the Garden of Eden, God gave Adam and Eve instructions for obedience and outlined the consequences for disobedience. However, one day the couple faced temptation and chose to disobeyed God. It was not until Adam and Eve learned that they could deliberately enter upon and even provoke sexual activity in themselves that they were cursed and cast out of Eden. God commanded them not to eat from the tree of knowledge of good and evil but the serpent enticed them with the desire for more knowledge. The couple already possessed a huge knowledge but did not realize that what they knew was sufficient. They succumbed to temptation and disobeyed God and their disobedience yield catastrophic consequences. Once their eyes were opened, Adam and

Eve no longer perceived good and evil from the perspective of righteousness but from the vantage of sin. It distanced their relationship with God. God banished them from the garden, condemned them and their generations of offsprings to physical death and promised them a life of labour and sorrow.

This act also established enemity between Humankind and Satan. All human beings as descendants of Adam inherited a sin nature at birth. Adam's death blood runs through our spiritual veins. The most profound codes for living crumble under the influence of our sin nature.

SOWING AND REAPING (CAUSES AND EFFECTS)

God created man with wits and equipped him with a free will, thus man is a free moral agent and NOT A ROBOT. Therefore whatever sins he committed so shall hc rcap. A man is the creator of his own fate and even in his foetal life he is affected by the dynamics of the works of his prior existence. Whether confined in a mountain fasting or lulling on the bossom of a sea, whether secured in his mother's lap or held high above her head. A man cannot fly away from the effects of his own deeds. Whatever is to befall a man at any particular age, time, will surely overtake him then and on that date. The same applies to knowledge acquired by a man in his prior birth, wealth given away in his charity in his prior existence and works done by him in a previous reincarnation which goes ahead of his soul in its sojourn. The results and effects of which has brought man into his present body and has to be paid off in this life. The reactions of these sins (karmas) comes to us unexpectedly and unperceived and we have no control over them. This is the unalterable laws of nature owing to which this universe exists. Ignorance of these laws is no excuse.

The laws of causes and effects which is the root causes of physical existence and the clever device of nature to maintain this existence. The universal laws sees to it that we are paid an eye for an eye and tooth for tooth, in the shape of joy and suffering, it is the goading whip in the hidden hands of nature.The mind contracts sins (karmas), puts a covering on the soul and rules the body through the organs and the senses, although it is the soul that impacts strength to the mind, therefore control of the mind is the first step to spirituality, in other words victory over the mind is victory over the world. Similarly; the same way the sins of Adam and Eve affect us, is the same way our parents sins affect us even though that we may not be aware of this. The results of some of these we reap before we die or transferred to our offsprings.By destiny and fate, two person cannot have the same mission on Earth and by that same destiny and fate, some people are richly endowed while others have very little or nothing. All this depends on successive incarnations in connections with ones deeds in previous lifetime. There is a big connection between Bible education and reincarnation and any attempt to separate them will create more confusion. For example, the Bible says that when Elias was returning from meditation- that's from prayer house- then little children saw him and followed after him chanting, Elias bald head, Elias bald head, so in his anger, Elias called up the beasts and the beasts came from nowhere and devoured these children. Because as a powerful man of God his words have creative powers and to speak is to create. The Bible put it this way: (Matthew 17 : 12-13) But I say unto you, Elias has come already and they knew him not, but have done unto him whatever they listed. Likewise shall also the son of ... 13)

Then the disciples understood that he spake unto them of John the Baptist and the second side of the story was recorded in the book of (Matthew 14 : 1-11. In another event of causes and effects read (Genesis 25 : 22-34 ; 33 : 1-16) and also (2Samuel 6 : 1-17) ; his great sin in converting Bathsheba (2Samuel 6 : 1-17) ; rebellion of his son Absalom.

THE MYSTERIOUS TRANSMISSION INFLUENCE

A single inherited gene can impact our health for good or ill. However, long before we were introduced to the science of genetics, it was an acceptable metaphysical principle that when people conceive children everything within them (ie) physical health, mental and emotional states and spiritual condition is combined between them and delivered to the unborn child.

Since we are born of man and woman, when our forefathers conceived children, if their inner and outer states were impure or weakened or in any way affected negatively by their world, these impurities were passed to their children ending ultimately with us, the present generation. This successive transmission of influences is not, of course, always bad since good influences can also be transmitted but if the negative outweighed the positive in our ancestry, then it is our burden to cope with the result in some measure. This does not mean that we should blame our parents or their parents, etc for they too suffered both the positive and negative effects of this process. The cleft in your chin, the swagger in your walk and your aptitude for maths are all inherited from your parents DNA. So too, do you inherited some unwelcome genes in the form of a predisposition to certain illnesses. We have long known that these genes are fixed within your physical being, unchanged and intact to be passed on the future generations. But, do you have any control over them? And can you alter your genes before passing them on to your offsprings? From conception, a new foetus is made up of 50 percent DNA from each parent respectively, and its genetic mould is formed and sealed. Fifty percent of its DNA will then be passed on to his or her future offsprings. This is called genetic determinism and has dominated the science of genetics for a long time. A major breakthrough in science was the mapping of the human genome in the early 1990s.The blueprint for human life was deciphered, revealing the layout of all 30,000 genes making up a strand of human DNA based on all that science has taught us, up till now the genome we inherited from our parents seems to determine how we look, how we perform and what illnesses we may incurred.But,once again,science may be about to turned on its head with a new science called epigenetic, which means control above genes.Think of it like this:the genome is the powerful DNA hardware within each and every cell; epigenetic is the software controlling the expression and manifestation of these genes, telling our genes how, when and where to work.The truth is that it takes hundreds of genes to be activated or turned on and then expressed in a particular way for an illness to occur. Lifestyle factors are thought to contribute more than 70 percent of what makes us ill. With this new science, we may have even more control over illness.We may be born with mutant genes, but we seem to have the power to rewrite their expression and therefore prevent the manifestation of disease. Epigenetic is now revealing that genes may in fact be flexible. We now know that 20 percent of our genome is fixed, such as the color of our eyes and how tall we grow. but, the other 80 percent can be amended by life circumstances and choices. So, not doing anything about your smoking, alcohol overindulgence, excess weight and unrelenting stress is not just a threat to your personal health, it is an assault on the legacy of your genome, which you will pass on to the generations to come. From the moment we are born and throughout our adults lives we accumulate experiences that causes us to act or react. These actions and reactions leave an imprint or mark in our bodies, minds and feelings, and penetrate to the soul overtime and the combined result can influence not only our attitudes and emotions, but what and how we think generally and whether we can believe, truly believe that we can rise above our present circumstances.We all know that the world can be both a beautiful and perilous place if, as we grow into our adult years, we have the misfortune of encountering painful relationships, difficulties; people may face in life. In the face of these obstacles, it has been shown that people with some measure of spirituality in their lives tend to recover better overall. Though the conventional definition of spiritual is religious or that which relates to recognized religion and its dogma, the society prefers to define spiritual in its more ancient definition, meaning a state of being relating to the soul and spirit, and an affinity with the source whether or not and to what degree, the spiritual element is present in our lives and is perhaps the single most important factor in helping us overcome the barriers to success in achieving what we want for ourselves. As the saying goes: With God Nothing Shall Be Impossible. This is perhaps the greatest of the truths, but also we must take responsibility for ourselves which is the test of life and an important part of why we exist in this world. Bear in mind; a vital point here is that even if we don't feel or recognize the action of these influence within us, they are there. Some work for us and some against us. It is little wonder then, that in the pursuit of a better life we can meet with struggle and disappointment more often than not, even when we know we have done nothing to derserve it. The Good new is that it does not have to be that way. We do not have to be puppets on a string at the mercy of the forces we were born with, or that foisted upon us from the outside. Despite the opposition, both subtle and obvious, within and without, we can overcome the difficulties and breakfree from the limitations these forces impose on us.

ASTROLOGY AND HOROSCOPES

We define predestination as the eternal design of God,whereby he determined what he wanted to do with each man. For he did not created them all equal, each and everyone has a special purpose and mission to accomplish based on past lives deeds. Nothing in this world happens by accident, and for detailed explanations let's take a look at the science of astrology and horoscope. Astrology is the study of the celestial bodies and their apparent influences on the life and evolution of man. It could be called the study of star lore, a study of the wisdom of the universe. Every soul has its particular lesson to learn, but also follows a path of development and unfoldment upon which it meets the same problems that have confronted saints and seers from the beginning of time. These symbolic trials are part of the orderly process of unfoldment of the universe within every soul. A study of astrology compels one to accept that a wonderful plan is being worked out in every life, a plan which can be traced in the heavens at birth. A child's time of birth is not an accident by a divine law. A baby takes its first breath at the exact moment when the planets are in the positions which will bring to that soul the experience it needs for the unfoldment of its God-like powers. At the level of individual human experience those who take the trouble to trace out working of the signs and planets in their own lives and those of their family and friends are regularly fascinated by the way in which the laws of the heavens are reflected in their lives They examine especially when they can see some major events which affect the life of the whole family or group shown by the progressed planets of all concerned. One can study the biography of any great personality in conjunction with the horoscope, and again find that every crucial development in life is mirrored by the planets positions in the heavens at birth, and by their subsequent progression. In any chart,the astrology will find the reflected direction of the individual life, the work they will be drawn to, the type of partner they will marry or work with, the physical weaknesses to which they may be subjected, their hobbies and general interests, and their attitude on money and possession. In relationships to problems with human relationships,a study of the birth charts of the protagonists helps to reveal the cause of the conflict and how they are affected.Thus the pattern of the heavens is reflected in our lives.The science of astrology is based upon well-known hermetic axiom, As Above, So Below, As Below, So Above:In other words, the positions and movements of the stars and planets in the heavens reflect what is happening within our inner universe. An astrological chart can therefore tell us a good deal about why we have incarnated and what we are trying to achieve in our lives, both in terms of lessons we are learning and what we are attempting to accomplish. It sheds light on our path.This is why astrology can be so useful to us .It encapsulates in symbolic form all the various tests and experiences through which we undergo and helps us to understand them. Now, remember that the three wise men that came to visit JESUS at birth were astrologers. Everyone who accepts any form of astrology regardless to what degree, shares one belief. Whether or not the stars actually cause things to happen or directly affect people or events…there is definitely a relationship between our lives and the stars influence. Most people think of astrologers as Horoscopes and predictions.The average person, being selfish creature wants to know about himself or herself and what is going to happen to them in their own little personal world. So, they are actually seeking fortune-telling and would be as well off with some charlatan gypsy with a few tea leaves in a dirty cup… as if a tea leaf had clairvoyant powers.Unfortunately,some so-called astrologers go into such quackery to make a few miserable dollars. This practice is, of course scorned by sincere and serious students of astrology. Understand one thing, here at the beginning….astrology is not prophesying. Astrology does not tell what is sure to happen. It tells what might happen at certain different times. These are not the same thing. Look at it this way, if the weatherman says that it will probably rain. You would be wise to carry an umbrella. If a farmer was given warning of a severe winter storm coming up, he would be a fool to put his livestock out to summer pasture. On the other hand, on a balcony summer day with more sunshine predicted it would be safe to go on a picnic. A ship without a compass might arrive at its destination but the chances would be better with the compass and a good map. But there is more to it than this. If your future could be exactly predicted there would be nothing to do but to reconcile yourself to what is going to happen and accept it and let it go at that. But if you know the dangers to which you might be exposed, you can take precautions to overcome them. If you had plans to do something that would benefit you, wouldn't you?It is good to know that all the outside forces were favourable to your undertakings or endeavour.All competent astrologers agree that the prediction of events to come is not one of astrologers strongest point. The most important and most dependable powers that astrology offers is the ability to understand your own as well as other peoples character or their potential strengths or weaknesses. Just think what an advantage to be able to anticipate the attitude or reaction of other people by your knowledge of their temperament and character and natural disposition. You will be able to tell what they are apt to do in any given situation, better than that person himself. You will also be able to control your own temperament and cope with your own problems.Let me correct a blunder by the commercial horoscope preparers that, unfortunately is widely acceptable by a gullible public. A horoscope is not an astrological chart. Everyone born in the same month does not have same life or destiny and does not need the same advice. The highly imaginative but unreliable writers of most of the drivel in the horoscope columns will say: Are you born between May 22nd and June 21nd? Then you are a Gemini. Or is your birthday between January 22 and November 10? Then you are an Aquarius. This is ridiculous. Any astrologer worth listening to, knows that you can be born in the month of Aquarius and yet be a Sagittarian. In addition to the zodiac sign the position of the sun and the moon at the time of your birth and the place where you are born must be considered. This is why the astrological chart is so important. The positions of the planets are changing constantly… Actually, they are changing minute by minute, so to attempt to give the same analysis and advice to everyone born under the same sign of the zodiac is absurd. This practice is the weakness of newspapers and radios. Astrology attempts to tell all Sagittarians and Leos and Virgos and so on around the zodiac what that day or week or month holds in store for them, obviously, most people don't take their advice too seriously.

WESTERN NEGATIVE INFLUENCE

The Westerners had divided the lands of the Earth into continents, countries and partitioned each nations-land with separating boundaries. But no one can divide the sun, moon and the sky. The same sun shines to all nations. There is one undivided heaven for everyone. We all cry when we are sad and we all laugh when we are happy. We are born the same way and when we die our soul shall return back to the same God. There is no denying the fact that God blessed the Westerners with more technological inventions than the black race. Alas, it was the Westerners that colonized, re-civilized, educated, and brain-washed the entire black race into religious dogmas. It was also true that all the greatest spiritual societies, Anglican churches, Protestant churches, Catholic churches, Peace movements, Human rights organisations, moral schools, renowned universities and colleges, school of thoughts and the highest moral educational systems had their headquarters based in the land of the Westerners. The Westerners willfully misused and abused these priceless potentials that the Divine Creator endowed them with, without any confinement to immoral traits, thus abusing the freedom of choice. Obviously, the Westerners were supposed to be the moral pillars of standard behaviours and a foundation of faith in today's world. Appreciative comments like: God bless you, is almost non-existent in Westerners' communities except for handful of them that are true Christians. I personally have had several encounter with some Westerners who don't believe in God, Some of which are doctors, engineers, lawyers and bankers and not illiterates. Now can you imagine how hard it will be for such people to forgive you when you unintentionally offend them? It is mostly in the lands of the Westerners that people terminate their lives because of trivial issues. Suicide is wide spread among the Westerners and when they get angry over a minor issues, believe me, the Gates of Hell will get lose(you cannot predict what would happen next) their next line of actions could be deadly. One day, in the course of a telephone conversation between me and one of my penpal who lived in United States, he told me that he and his father are in New York but had not seen each other in the last eighteen months ago except that they often talked to each other via telephone. Now let's turn back the hands of time to the era of the slave trade. The Westerners knew God. They also knew good and bad things but they consciously did horrible and abominable things to the black race. They forcefully captured, raped, tortured, impregnated, killed and burnt so many black people that were held captive. Does that make them good or bad people? Inevitably,they must atone for their past and present evil deeds. The Bible says that as a man sow, so he reap. So they must atone for their evil atrocities. Worst yet, in the name of civilization and modernization the Westerners created unholy lifestyles labelled: homosexuals, bestiality,sodomite and a host of others. Now tell me, how a normal human being would get married to the same sex. This is absolutely nonsense. The Westerners civilization are really demonic. They are really anti-God and Anti-nature. These evil acts are inglorious things that debases Humanity, for a man that is created in the image and likeness of God to indulge in such a diabolic lust. It is also sad to know that some Catholic priests and Anglican leaders are homosexuals. Little more than a generation ago such actions would have caused moral outraged. Today, we are bombarded with sexual imagery from every conceivable angle and pornography has planted itself firmly in the mainstream. How times have changed. Not long ago the very idea of gays or lesbians openly cohabiting was a moral outrage. The Bible (Romans 14: 12) says; Each of us will render an account for himself to GOD. This Bibilical statement is factual and must be respected.It is not something to be taken lightly or glossed over. If the politicians had treated millions under their care like animals dispatched to slaughter, then what colon of religion or ethnics could prevent men from treating others with the ferocity of jungle beasts…? The slaughter of the First World War (1914-18) toughly debased the value of human life. It was following the acceptance of the evolution theory that a real de-moralization ensued because most Westerners held that man is simply a higher form of animal life. The First World War had a devastating effect upon people's sense of morality. The older generation was completely discredited in everything - its politics, its dress, its sexual moves. Nations were making fearsome weapons of destruction, snapping the world out of the Depression but plunging it into suffering and horror beyond human imagination. The fact that, God is invisible doesn't mean that God do not exist as most Westerners thinks and believed. Electric current flows inside the electric cable and you do not see the electric current flowing through it. Therefore, the fact that it is invisible and cannot be seen does not mean that it does not exist. The same as air or wind or signal and radio wave. The Holy Spirit of God in you, is your conscious ,that blames you when you do something wrong and encourages you when you do something right.When sleeping at night, your heart does not sleep or rest at that time. It is awake and beats. Non-stop. That is the breath of life force in you which is the Divine presence of God in you, because if your heart is asleep as you are sleeping then you are dead. Therefore, there is no reason to say that there is no God.

In 2008, when financial crises hit the economy of the Europeans and equally the United States of America, which brought them to their knees, the so-called strong nations or G8 wept like infants. Their human wisdom failed coupled with their sophisticated technological know-how. The most powerful nations and their coalition countries trembled – just in a breath. Why wouldn't they save themselves overnight?. At that period all the biggest, richest, largest banks and car companies and other businesses crumbled including all their political strongholds were brought to zero. Who would save them?

That reminds me of the Bible chapter(John 3:16) that says: For God so loved the world that he gave his only begotten son... That was a period that they will never forget in the history of this world. Must I remind them to add that event in their so-called Guinness book of records.

The Westerners had channeled 50 percent of their material resources for the sole purpose of manufacturing fearsome mass destructive weapons.They also sold these weapons to other countries when one country challenged another. The next thing is war that will eventually broke out- the countries that manufactured arms sends out their proposals of selling arms to the countries at war thereby enriching themselves while billions are dying including the innocent ones. They are also responsible for most of the wars and elections malpractices, rebels, and other forms of violence that had invaded African countries like: Congo, Rwanda, Angola, Sierra-Leone, Liberia, Nigeria, Togo, Somalia, Ivory-Coast etc,where they sold arms legally or illegally to some top political leaders and government officials. They are directly or indirectly supporting wars. The big question is: Why do they sell arms to rich men in AFRICA.This is a vital question that needs to be answered because that is the root causes of wars in African countries through rebels or oppositions or political leaders. There is another big lesson that I need everyone to learn. In war there is no winner. All are losers because if you killed my fifty soldiers and I killed your twenty soldiers .We have all lost, so no one is a winner.Even if arms are to be sold to African nations- it must be on conditions and this must be for national protective interests and to combat criminals and armed robbery within the national territory and for defence of national rights. No individual licensed or unlicensed should have the legal right to sell arms because everyman has his price , so goes the saying. They also invented electromagnetic virus which they transmitted to computers and internet emails and consequently caused a great damage to computer end users and in turn, the end users were compelled to buy anti-virus software made by the same Westerners to disinfect and protect their computers . This is an indirect way of acquiring money dubiously.The same with HIV virus, vaccinations and drugs.

LIFE AND ABORTION

Is life precious or cheap? Since man is made in the image of God, the taking of a man's life is the destruction of the most precious and most holy thing in the world. The price of life is too high and the protection of life is a fundamental element in the law. The scientific protection and use of embryonic stem cells presupposes the killing of the embryo. The embryo is truly a human living entity, and therefore deserves human dignity and protection of life; therefore the doctors should be prohibited from performing any intervention on the embryo that kills it. The price of life is too high. Life saving research cannot be bought at the cost of terminating another human life that also has human dignity and merits protection. God considers the life of a child to be precious even in the very earliest stages of development. Believe it or not, abortion is a serious sin tantamount to murder and this type of practice is not in harmony with the Divine principle of respect for life.

THE MIRACLE OF CONCEPTION.

The development of all the parts of an embryo begins at conception when the ovum or egg cell of the woman is fertilized by the sperm cell of a man. New advances in technology have enabled scientists to observe the amazing changes that take place in the nucleus making up the DNA (deoxyribonucleic acid) of the father and mother combined to create a human life that never existed before. That original single cell begins the truly miraculous process of constructing a fully formed human. The nature of this construction is determined by our genes which are segments of DNA.These control virtually everything about us, they determine our height, facial features, eyes and hair colour and thousands of other traits. Afterward, as that original cell divides, the complete genetic blueprint is duplicated into every new cell. Amazingly, each of these is programmed to develop into whatever kind of cell is needed. This includes, heart tissue, brain cells, bone, skin, and even transparent tissue for our eyes. The initial programming of a unique new person has understandably often been referred to as a miracle.

The human being is fully programmed for human growth and development for his or her entire life. There can no longer be any doubt that each human being is totally unique from the very beginning of his or her life at fertilization. From the time of conception in the womb, the child is not just another part of the mother's tissue, but a separate person. The mom's body views it ″As foreign objects″. It would be quickly rejected were it not for the protective wall created in the mother's womb. This new human life separated from the mother by protective housing is a person with a unique DNA fingerprint. Some argue that a woman's body spontaneously aborts many fertilized eggs because of abnormalities, so why shouldn't a doctor be able to abort a pregnancy, yet there is a difference between spontaneous death and deliberate homicide. In one South American country, 71 out of 1,000 children die within their first year just because so many die prematurely. Would it be acceptable to kill a child under the age of one? Of course not. Significantly, the Bible describes a human life as existing in the womb.

The psalmist David wrote concerning God:Your eyes saw me even the embryo of me, and in your book all it's parts were down written (psalms 139 :16) David does not simply say an embryo but "the embryo of me" thus accurately revealing that David's life began when he was conceived, long before his birth. Under inspiration by God, David also revealed that at conception the development of his body parts were according to a plan, or detailed written instructions, which made him the person he was. Note that the Bible does not say a woman conceives a piece of tissue.Instead, it states that: An able-bodied man has been conceived. (Job 3.3) This too indicates that according to the Bible, a child exist as a person from the time of his conception. Yes, that is when human life begins.

PROOF THAT GOD EXISTS

Your heart functions constantly and capably without your direction. In fact, you cannot consciously direct it. Your heart is only one of many parts of your body that actually works inspite of what you might wish it to do. Obviously, if these parts of your body that are not consciously directed by you – heart, lungs, kidneys and stomach - were to depend on your conscious direction in order to act, the moment you went to sleep, you would be dead. You cannot see thought neither can you see a radio wave. But radio wave are there carrying their messages across oceans,over mountains, and through thick walls.You cannot see God too. Do not be misled by the assertions of people who deny that there is no God. According to them, blind impersonal forces of nature made you. They claim that far from being made in the image of God, you are not different from the other animal life on this Earth. Does it really make sense to you that life got here simply by chance or blind force? Do you find it difficult to believe that God considers you – just one individual, precious? Then note what the prophet Isaiah wrote about the billions of stars in the billions of galaxies in the vast universe around us. We read: Raise your eyes high up and see. Who has created these things? It is the one who is bringing forth the army of them even by number, all of whom he calls even by name.Due to the abundance of dynamic energy, he also being vigorous in power, not one of them is missing (Isaiah 40: 26). Do you appreciate what that means? Our Milky way galaxies- of which our Solar System is only a part contains at least 100 billion stars and how many other galaxies are there? No one knows for sure, but some estimates put the figure at 125 billion. What a staggering number of stars by name. Yet, the Bible tells us that God of the universe knows each of stars by name .But someone may object,and say just knowing the names of billions of stars or billions of people does not necessarily mean caring about them individually. A computer with sufficient memory capacity could register the names of billions of people. Yet no one would suggest that the computer cares about any of them. The Bible shows however that God not only knows the names of billions of people but also cares about them as individuals."Throw all your anxiety upon him", wrote Peter, because he cares for you (1 Peter 5: 7). Jesus Christ states: Do not two sparrows sell for a coin of small value? Yet not one of them will fall to the ground without your father's knowledge. But the very hairs of your head are all numbered. Therefore, has no fear: you are worth more than many sparrows (Matthew 10: 29-31) Notice that Jesus did not say that God would simply be aware of what happened to sparrows but to men. He said: You are worth more than many sparrows. Why are you worth more? Because you are made in the image and likeness of God with the potentials for displaying moral, intellectual and spiritual qualities that reflect God's own elevated qualities (Gen 1: 26-27).

YOU ARE WONDERFULLY MADE

When you reflect on the remarkable abilities of various animals? do you sometimes feel a twinge of envy?Perhaps you wish that you could soar like an albatross, swim like a dolphin, see like an eagle, or run like a cheetah.Yes, animals have some amazing abilities. But so do we .Indeed, the human body has been described as the perfect machine. Of course , we are much more than a machine. We have creativity, curiosity, imagination, and ingenuity – qualities that move us to devise machines that enable us to do virtually anything we set our minds to. We can fly, even beyond the speed of sound; navigate above or below the surface of a vast oceans; peer into the living cell; and design medicines, diagnose and treat diseases. Even with little or no external assistance, healthy, well-trained humans are capable of doing astonishing things. At the Olympic Games, for example, gymnasts, high divers, ice-skaters, skiers, and others perform amazing feats with a level of agility, artistry, creativity, and grace that leave audiences enthralled. Do you appreciate the special gifts that you have as a human. Granted, you may not be an Olympic athlete, but you have a gifts for which to be thankful. An ancient Bible writer expressed his appreciation to God in song :I shall laud you because in a fear-inspiring way iam wonderfully made.(psalms 139:14)Why not think about the statement as you consider the articles that follow? They will examine in more detail some of the wonders of the human body, as well as other far more important traits that make us truly unique.

APPRECIATE YOUR SPECIAL GIFTS

The human body is outstandingly versatile. No animal has the sheer range of abilities that we human do. One reason for our versatility is our upright stance, which not only expands our area of vision but also frees our arms and hands for any number of tasks. Imagine how our activities would be curtailed if we had to walk on all fours.

Another asset is our highly sophisticated sensory system, which will be the focus of this article. The system includes the hands, the ears, the eyes, and, of course, our exceptional brain. Let's look at these individually .

THE HUMAN HAND

Our hands are beautiful instruments of amazing precision. With them we can thread a needle or swing an axe, paint a portrait or play the piano. Our hands are also highly sensitive. Even a brief touch may reveal whether a substance is fur, paper, skin, metal water, or wood. Yes, our hands are much more than implements for grasping and manipulation. They are also a source of knowledge about our world and they are a means of conveying warmth and affection.Why is a human hand so adept, so expressive, so sensitive, and so versatile? The reasons are many.Our two hands have a total of more than fifty bones, about a quarter of all the bones in the body. The intricate assembly of the parts of the hand-the bones, the joints, the ligaments-gives the human hand extraordinary flexibility.The hand has an opposable thumb mounted on a saddle joint, an ingenious configuration of two saddle-shaped surfaces at right angles of each other. The joint, along with the associated muscles and other tissues, gives the thumb amazing flexibility and strength.

(1) Three sets of muscles control the hand. The two most powerful sets-the extensors and the flexors-are in the forearm and operate the fingers by means of tendons. How bulky and unwieldy the hand would be if these muscles were located in it .The third set , much smaller, which does lie within the hand, gives the fingers precision of movement.

(2) Your fingers are, in effect, living sensors – the fingertips having about 2,500 receptors in just one square centimeter. Moreover, the function, enabling you to feel texture, temperature, wetness, vibration, pressure, and pain. As a result, the human finger is the most sensitive touch sensor known.

THE HUMAN EAR

Although some animals can hear sound frequencies beyond the range of human hearing, the combination of a human's ears and brain is a formidable one. Our hearing enables us to determine loudness, pitch, and tone and to approximate the direction and distance of a sound source.

The frequency range of a healthy human ear is roughly 20 to 20,000 hertz, or cycles of sound oscillation per second. The most sensitive region is in the 1,000 to 5,000 hertz range. Moreover, we may be able to detect a change of just one hertz from, say,440 hertz to 441 hertz. Indeed, a healthy ear is so sensitive that it can detect sounds when the vibration, or to-and-fro movement of the air at the eardrum is less than the diameter of an atom. Ear drum vibrations are amplified mechanically by lever action and are transferred to the inner ear by means of the ossicles-tiny bones known as the hammer, the anvil, and the stapes. But what if your ears are suddenly struck by a deafening sound? In that event, they have a built-in protective mechanism in the form of muscle action that adjusts the ossicles to reduce the force of the sound. However, the ears are not equipped to deal with prolonged loud noise. Such exposure can permanently damage the hearing. Your auditory system also helps you to detect a sound source.The secret lies in a number of factors including the shell-like shape of the outer ear, its grooves,the separation of the two ears, and some computational brilliance on the part of your brain. Thus, if the intensity of a sound fades just slightly from ear to ear or if the sound reaches one ear just 30 millionths of a second before it reaches the other, your brain will promptly point your eyes toward the sound source. Imagine if you had to make all those computations consciously. To be sure, you would have to know how to use very advanced mathematics-device at lightning speed. If an engineer were to design a hearing system that came even remotely close to the one your creature gave you, he would receive many accolades. Yet, how often do you hear people give due credit to God for his awesome works?

THE HUMAN EYE

Some researchers estimate that people who can see well gain approximately 80 percent of their information about the world through their eyes.

In combination with our brain, our eyes enable us to see in full colour, to track moving objects and images smoothly, to recognize patterns and shapes, and to see in varying degrees of light.The latter involves a number of complementary mechanisms. For example, the pupil can expand from 1.5 millimeters to 8 millimeters in diameter, resulting in a possible 30-fold increase in the amount of light entering the eye.The light then passes through the lens, which focuses it onto the retina, concentrating the light energy by a factor of 100,000 times. So never look directly at the sun with the naked eye.The retina , in turn houses two types of photoreceptors-cones approximately 6 million which give us colour vision and high resolution , and rods(120-140 million), which are more than a thousand times as sensitive as the cones and help us to see in dim light. Indeed, under optimal conditions, a rod can detect a single photon, or elementary particle of light. Engineers often design cameras, scanners, and computers, along with compatible software.

But the degree of intergration and the level of sophistication attained are vastly inferior to those of our sensory system .Ask youself, "Is it reasonable to attribute our vastly superior living sensory system to blind chance"?

THE HUMAN BRAIN

With astonishing efficiency, the brain decodes the streams of signals pouring in through the nerves from the sense organs. Moreover, it links these signals with details stored in its memory. Thus a certain smell may immediately trigger the brain to retrieve a long-forgotten experience or event. And if you see just a small part of something familiar –the tip of your cats tail , for example –your brain will fill in the missing details so that you know your cat is nearby.

Of course, your brain was not preprogrammed with images of cats, just as it was not preprogrammed with the smell of a rose or the sound of running water . Your brain learned these associations.The experiences of people who were born blind but have been given the ability to see, perhaps through surgery , make this evident. Their brain had to learn to interpret the flood of visual signals now flowing to it. How do such people fare?

They soon report the ability to detect colour , motion, and forms. But after that, progress varies.

OUR UNIQUE SOLAR SYSTEM (CHANCE OR PURPOSE?)

Many factors combined to make our part of the universe unique. Our Solar System is located between two of the Milky Ways spiral arm in a region that has relatively few stars. Nearly all the stars that we can see at night are so far from us; that they remain mere points of light when viewed through the largest telescopes. Is that how it should be? If our Solar System were close to the center of the Milky Way, we would suffer the harmful effects of being among a dense concentration of stars. Earth orbit for example would likely be perturbed, and that would dramatically affect human life. As it is, the Solar System appears to have just the right position in the galaxy to avoid this and other dangers such as overheating when passing through gas clouds and being exposed to exploding stars and other sources of deadly radiation. The sun is an ideal type of star for our needs. It is steady burning, long-lived and neither too large nor too hot. The vast majorities of stars in our galaxy are much smaller than our sun and provide neither the right kind of light nor the right amount of heat to sustain life on an earthlike planet. In addition, most stars are gravitationally bound to one or more other stars and revolve around one another. Our sun, by contrast, is independent. It is unlikely that our Solar System would remain stable if we had to contend with the gravitational force of two or more suns.

Another factor that makes our Solar System unique is the location of the giant outer planets that have almost circular orbits and pose no gravitational threat to the inner terrestrial planets. Instead, the outer planets fulfill the protective function of absorbing and deflecting dangerous objects .Asteroids and comets hit us but not excessively so, thanks to the presence of giant gas planets such as Jupiter beyond us. The role of the Moon since ancient times, our moon has filled mankind with wonders. It has inspired poets and musicians. For instance, an ancient Hebrew poet describes the moon as "being firmly established for time indefinite" and as a faithful witness in the skies-(Psalm 89: 37). Tidal movements are thought to be fundamental to ocean currents which, in turn, are vital for our weather patterns.

Another key purpose of our moon is that its gravitational force stabilizes Earth's axis with respect to Earth's plane of orbit around the sun. Without the moon, the inclination of Earth's axis would wobble over long periods of time from nearly (0 degrees to 85 degrees). Images if Earth's axis had no tilt. We would miss the delightful change of seasons and suffer from a shortage of rain. The Earth's tilt also prevents temperatures from becoming too extreme for us to survive. We owe our present climate stability to an exceptional event: the presence of the moon, yet another function of the Earth's natural satellite. How is one to explain the concurrence of multiple factors that make life on Earth not only possible but also enjoyable? There appear to be only two alternatives. The first is that all these realities are not the causual product of aimless chance. The second is that there is some intelligent purpose behind it. Thousands of years ago, the Holy Bible stated that our universe was conceived and crafted by a creator-Almighty God. If that is true, it means that the conditions that exist in our Solar System are a product, not a chance, but of deliberate design.The Creator left us with a report, so to speak of the steps he took to make life on Earth possible. It might surprise you to know that even though this report is some 3,500 years old, the events in universal history described in it basically correspond to what scientists believe must have taken place. This report is contained in the Bible book of Genesis. Consider what it says: The genesis accounts of creation. In the beginning God created the heavens and the Earth. (Genesis 1: 1) The Bible's opening words refer to the creation of our Solar System including our planet, as well as that of the stars in the millions of galaxies that make up our universe. According to the Bible, at one time the Earth's surface was formless.There were no continents and no productive land. The next words highlight what scientists say is the most important requirements for a life sustaining planet-an abundance of water. God's spirit was moving to and fro over the surface of the waters (Genesis 1: 2) For surface water to remain liquid , a planet must be the right distance from the sun. Mars is too cold, Venus is too hot, Earth is just right for the growth of vegetation, and there must be sufficient light. And significantly, the Bible account reports that during an early creative period, God caused the sun's light to penetrate dark clouds of water vapour that enveloped the ocean like a swaddling band around a baby (Genesis 1: 3-5). In the text verses of Genesis, we read that the creator produced what the Bible calls an expanse. (Genesis 1: 6-8) this expanse is filled with gases making up the Earths atmosphere. The Bible then explains that God changed the formless surface of the Earth to make dry land. (Genesis 1: 9-10) He evidently caused the Earth's crust to buckle and move. As a result, deep troughs evidently may have been formed and continents pushed out of the ocean (Psalm 104: 6- 8) At some unspecified time in the Earth's past, God created microscopic algae in the oceans. Using energy from the sun, these self-reproducing one-celled organisms began to convert carbon dioxide into food while releasing oxygen into the atmosphere.This marvelous process was hastened during a third creative period by the creation of vegetation that eventually covered the land. Thus, the amount of oxygen in the atmosphere increased, which would make it possible for man and animals to sustain their lives by breathing (Genesis 1: 11, 12)

To make the land productive, the Creator caused a variety of micro-organism to live in the soil. (Jeremiah 51: 15) These tiny creatures break down dead matter, recycling elements that plants use to grow. Special types of soil bacteria capture nitrogen from the air and make this vital element available to plants so that they can grow.

Amazingly, an average handful of fertile soil may contain six billion micro organisms. (Genesis 1: 14-19) describes the forming of the sun, moon, and the stars in a third creative period. At a glance, this might seem to contradict the forgoing scriptural explanation. Bear in mind, however, that Moses, the writer of Genesis penned the creation account from the viewpoint of an Earthly observer, had one been present. Apparently, the sun, moon, and the stars became visible through Earth's atmosphere at that time.

The Genesis account assigns the appearance of sea creatures to a fifth creative period and that of terrestrial animals and of man to a sixth creative period (Genesis 1 : 20-31) All these features are absent on Mars, Venus, and our other planetary neighbours. Aren't the product of earth pleasurable?

One must know God to learn Divine knowledge. You must be pure to the extent that all of your efforts are concentrated on only one thing. You must have a close spiritual union with the Supreme power. You cannot start with selfish, material thoughts cluttering your mind. With this purity of purpose the quest becomes simple and the goal will be reached. We believe in one GOD, the fountain-head, the source of life. It is pitiful how many so-called well educated highly trained people do not know who they really are. They do not recognize that all that they are… that everything they receive mentally or physically, is a gift from God our Father. Sometimes they even have the misguided audacity to question the very existence of a Supreme being… God. If you ever have doubts that God is real and that the awesome Divine powers are always in control think of the following and pray to God through his only begotten son Jesus Christ. If the Earth's crust were just 20 feet thicker or thinner,if the ocean floor were a little deeper or shallower than it is… no man or beast or plant would remain alive. The sun gives warmth and light but if it were to move the least bit closer or the slightest bit farther away,for just one second in all the billions of days of its steady rounds… there would be no more life. Everything and everyone on Earth would be burned or frozen. In fact, there would be no more Planet Earth. It is a miracle how the myriad of different plants capture light from the sun and convert it to use by all living things to feed upon or receive shelter or just enjoying nature's beauty can only be a part of a magnificently Divine plan. Haven't you ever wondered about the regular certainty of the seasons? Summer, autumn, winter and Spring. They are engineered by God who dependably turns the Earth on its axis. The axis is always tilted at exactly the right degree to arrange the seasons, year in and year out. The moon softly beautifies the night as it rides serenely high in the sky and also controls the ocean tides. But, if from its great distance, its pull on the tides were to deviate the tiniest bit, those useful tides would swamp the shores and all lands would be awash and lost. Look at the heavens. Billions upon billions of stars beautifully shining in limitless space. Each one in its own orderly orbit. None ever interfering with another. Who but God guides the birds in their unmarked flight or the fish in the trackless sea, back to where they were born to spawn and replenish the waters? Do you believe that these constant wonders are accidents? Who but God created love? God is love and love is God , love is all. For God so loved the world that he gave his only begotten son that whosoever believe in him should not perish but have everlasting life.

(John 3: 16) If you exist then God exist. You have been kissed by God to give you life. You were created by God's love. You are held in God's warm embrace. You can see millions of stars in the sky in the darkness of night but you cannot see the stars once the sun has come up. Yet you cannot say that the stars are not there in the daytime just because you cannot see them. You dare not say that there is no God simply because you cannot see God .Water is water, no matter where you find it. Different people have different names for it: water, aqua, eau, pani, H20 and so no. But regardless what it might be called in various places, it is the same material substance everywhere. It is the same with God. Some call the Divine presence, God, some say Jehovah. All these names plus many more. But whatever the name, the Divine presence is the same. Many people, too many in fact, spend their lives regretting and complaining because they are not wealthy or that they lack material possessions or that they have not found a congenial lover. But how many people weep because they have not met God? Yet anyone who seeks God will find him. Try for only three days and you will be successful. It is that easy.

THE GREAT LORD JESUS

A saviour was sent as a messenger of God in earthly form. He has duties similar to those of an ambassador or envoy of a mighty emperor or rulcr. When there is a problem or trouble in a far off province of the empire, the emperor or the ruler sends his envoy to strengthen things out. In the same manner, when there is a breakdown of moral values or a decline or neglect of righteousness or too much evil in the world, God sends an envoy… A Saviour. This special envoy enters earthly life and rises in one place and is known as Jesus Christ. Jesus came into the world to produce dramatic changes in the ways of the people of the earth. Jesus returned to a miserable, materialistic world of narrow-minded, ignorant people, willing to blindly accept the ideas and rules of a group of leaders who had neither conscience nor ideas. It was a world led by a few zealous hypocrites who were more interested in outward ceremonies than true spiritual wisdoms. To these misled people, the magnificent thoughts expounded by Jesus were almost unbelievable. All of his efforts were to promote happiness and the spiritual elevation of everyone from the very lowest to the most affluent. He eventually gave his life trying to change the social evils that beset the world and unfortunately some still exist, even to day. Why are our religious leaders and teachers unable to fully explain the true meanings of the parables and the symbolic messages? Because they do not completely understand the hidden fundamentals and principles of Jesus Christ. Many clergyman and teachers of all faiths are guilty of evading this situation. But the fact remain that Jesus was and is the greatest moral teacher the world has ever known. No preacher or speaker has the real meaning of His grand expressions. The best of most minister's sermons might be compared with Christ's least.But Jesus Christ's best rises above the minister's best, the very way that a magnificent cathedral towers over a beggars hut. Jesus gave a crass, material world a beautiful doctrine that changed the way of life of millions upon millions, yet even today it is known, understood and taught by very few churches. The true teachings of Jesus can only be properly used, in a personal or collective way by a few who have the desire and the will to become enlightened. In His gospel there are hidden meanings which not everyone understands? In all of his expressions there is only a hint of the prophesy of the destiny of Mankind. If the teachings were properly understood it would be easier for the people to live up to them. If they were lived up to, the whole world would be revolutionized. Many ministers and preachers imagine that they are capable but their inept efforts only add to the confused interpretations and create more questioning of the credibility by those who seek enlightenment. Jesus left the richest legacy.The spiritual treasures of the rarest soul that ever lived on Earth but it has been crushed on the cold stones of materialism.It is impossible to estimate what we owe Him. If you were to take from the world what He gave to thinking people, life would become a meaningless desert. Many ignorant people are apt to overrate the values of the ones in power. In the book of (Matthew 15: 14), Jesus says, let them alone; they be blind: leaders of the blind. And if the blind lead the blind ,they both shall fall into a pit. Who could disagree with that? Jesus knew the ways of life. He knew that nature cares neither for smile nor for tears. For life or death. The sun shines as pleasantly on coffins as on cradles. In many of the expressions of Jesus there is almost a kind of scorn, a hidden meaning in his days could not have been voiced without personal peril. That is the reason many of His sublime sayings and declarations are clothed in vague allegory; often resulting in misinterpretations. There is a story told about Jesus as follows: Jesus had said, if a man should do me wrong, I will return him my love. The more evil that comes from him, the more good shall go from me. A foolish man who had heard of Jesus Christ's returning good for evil, came to Jesus and insulted and abused him? Jesus kept silent until the man had finished his ranting and said; Man if a person would not accept a present that was offered to him, to whom does it belong? The man replied, Naturally, it would return to the person who offered it. So Jesus continued, Man, you ranted at me but I do not choose to accept your abuse and I ask you to keep it for yourself. Thus, it belongs to you. The foolish man could hardly reply, so Jesus went on, "An evil man who reproaches a good man is like someone who looks up and spit skyward".His spit doesn't reach at the sky but falls back and messes him up. Just the same, a virtuous man cannot be hurt but the misery that the evil one would inflict upon the righteous man. It would instead fall back to him. So it is clear, if you love God, with pure heart, you will also love everyone as your brothers and sisters who share this earth with you, because the same God that gave you life gave them life. They are as much a part of the divine plan as you are. God is the essence of life within each and everyone on earth: king, queen or pauper. The good, the wicked, the strong, the weak, the clever and dull, the rich and the poor. All are equally shined upon and washed by the same rain. All are loved by God. If you can say that you sincerely agree to these truths and try to live accordingly, you are a righteous person and you will not be harmed by evil.

GODS FOUR BASIC RULES

Love does not only mean a romantic experience, although it does include it. To be happy, one must have a generous and genuine capacity for love. Love of your God. Love of all your fellow beings. Love of life and living. Love of yourself and your family. **PEACE**, is the serenity of a contented life. Freedom from worry by knowing true security exist because God is aware of your needs and will provide for you and take care of you. **HAMONY** is your oneness with God, with nature and the universe. Compatibility with your surroundings, your friends and your companions and your neighbours. **JOY** is the seasoning for your life. It is the spiritual salt, spice and herbs that give life the flavor for a pleasant existence. How does one go about acquiring these qualities that will create a richer life? Let me take them one at a time. **LOVE**, is the strongest spiritual emotion. it is unselfish concern for others. It accepts another in loyalty and seeks good for others. It is the concern of GOD for man and all creatures. It is the human adoration of God. Love is both sweet and bitter. It is the sexual attraction between two lovers. It is the affection and tenderness between two people. It reaches its highest earthly degree of unselfishness in the love of a parent for a child. It is God manifest in a human being. Without love life would be a barren harsh wilderness. But remember, to find love, you must have love in your heart and be ready to offer it to whomever needs it or wants it. It is the willingness and desire to give without thought of reward. **PEACE**, civilized people have been endeavouring to find peace. That is peace between nations, tribes, and religious people. This peace brings freedom from war, bloodshed, strife and enslavement. Unfortunately, up to now the search for world peace has been unsuccessful. There has never been a time in history when there has not been a war of some sort going on somewhere on Earth. One of the bitterest religious wars, the crusades, lasted 174 years, from the year 1096 to 1270. Six times, religious armies swarmed out of Europe to attempt to wrestle control of the Holy Land from the Mohammedans. Today, nearly 700 years later, Muslems, Christians and Jews are still fighting one another for control and ravaging that very Holy Land they hold so dearly. In another part of the world, the British Isles, brother is killing brother in Ireland owing to catholic and Episcopal church procedures. The rites of the two denominations are so nearly the same that if an observer were to wander into either church's services, he could hardly tell which church he was attending. Yet much of that country is in bloody turmoil over this trifling difference.Where is the peace that churchmen preach about? The other type of peace is private or personal peace. Personal peace is the inner peace, peace of the soul, the spirit and mind. This is the wonderful condition that offers tranquility, even in a world of turmoil. You can achieve and enjoy this kind of peace by recognizing and believing in the security of the divine gift of Gods love to you and your love of God and all Gods creatures. This is the only dependable security.

Not material possessions.Material possessions are temporary. You can lose any or all of them, including money. You can lose your physical freedom. But your soul is your own, forever. It is the real you. It is blessed with the guarantee of eternal life, within the kingdom of God. Have you thanked God lately? **HARMONY** is to a great extent the result of love and peace. Harmony calls for a wholesome respect for yourself, your friends, your neighbours, the community where you live, your country,everyone with whom you have contact. You must relate, warmly to their hopes, their dreams, their aspirations. To find harmony, you must be free of hate, prejudice, envy, resentment and jealousy. You must be able to participate in another persons feelings and ideas. You must be able to sympathize with anothers distress and have a desire to help alleviate it and thus receive their good wishes. You should be truthful, fair and honest with yourself as well as others. You need a sense of humour and be able to laugh at your own mistakes for everyone makes mistake.You must be at peace with your Creator with whom you should maintain a warm spiritual relationship. Not necessarily in the sense of religious prayer. It is a personal relationship. You and God, God and you. You need all the attitudes of love, peace and joy. You should smile and be agreeable and grateful for the roses, not the thorns. They come together, you know. JOY, comes with a zest for living and the appreciation of the privilege of life. Have a sincere feeling of mutual well-being with others with whom you are sharing your part in the divine plan. Maintain a feeling of success, fulfillment and achievement. A pleasant disposition. A cheerful approach to life. There are always disappointments and frustrations, but they always pass away. They are the contrast that makes the good experiences sweeter and more enjoyable. Look for the beauty that is all around you. There was a silly limerick that went: As you go through life, brother… Whatever be your goal. Keep your eye upon the doughnut and not the hole. The Bible tells the story of David and Goliath.

You can read it in the book of Samuel, chapter 17. The Israelite soldiers took one look at the giant,(Goliath),and become almost paralyzed with fear, which was what the Philistine enemy had hoped to happen. And the Israelite soldiers began to flee, saying; Look at how big the Philistine is. How can you reach him to fight him? But the young shepherd, David went to King Saul and said: I will fight him. He is so big, how can I miss him? Maybe these my words are not exact words-the Bible tells it better but you get the idea. It is all in the way you look at it. These four sides of enrichment of life: love , peace,harmony and joy call for an unselfish attitude. You must give, if you expect to receive. If you follow the advice you will receive much more than you give. Believe it, the more you give of yourself, the more of the good life will come to you in return. So you are doing it as much for yourself as others. But keep in mind, if you project hate, envy, jealousy, resentment and anger, those thoughts will also return to you. You get what you give. You cannot plant rice and harvest beans. In your search for happiness, peace, love, and security and even earthly goods, there is a price to pay.If you cannot take the the time or are unwilling to take the trouble or participate or do your part in the effort, you cannot expect satisfying results. You may ask, what it is that you need to do. You must do more than to just stand with your hands out. You must pray at all times. This is not a hit and miss situation. You must pray daily. Not when the mood strikes you or when you are in trouble or when you are discouraged or depressed or as a last resort when all your own smart ideas have failed and most of all, not when you are seeking purely material things. If you have been in regular communication with God your life will never be the same.

SEX AND LUST

God created sex and called it good. He created the feminine figure and gave men eyes to see and admire. (beauty is in the eyes of the beholder) He made the masculine physique and persona, and gave woman desire for male companionship. God created testosterone and said it is not good for a man to be alone. We were engineered as sexual beings, not just for reproductive purposes but also for enriching our lives. The sphinx has the head of a man and the breasts of a woman. This is to demonstrate the power of the mind and the appeal of the body. Spiritual strength and carnal gratification. There is a reason and a use for both. But, in a well-adjusted human, the mind should be in control. Infact, with the mind in control the pleasure of the flesh is far more enjoyable. Again, you must decide if you, the divine being, or the animal nature within you is the master. But sexuality is also mental as well as physical. It is the mental consciousness and imagery of sex, not sex itself, that creates the ecstasy… The story goes as follows: It was not until Adam and Eve learned that they could deliberately enter upon and enjoy and even provoke sexual activity in themselves that they were cursed and cast out of Eden.Whether it is really love or only infatuation or just passion doesn't matter. More lives are distracted and disturbed and ambitions side-tracked by the personal relationship between a man and a woman than by anything else.These are strong emotions and not easy to control; but it is of tremendous importance that you try to handle them sensibly with a strong will. Obviously,you supposed to enjoy sex by choice not by chance. The relationship between two people that is capable of giving almost unendurable ecstasy is also one of the greatest causes of bitterness, heartbreak and frustration. Sexual experiences must be mental as well as physical in order to enter into one of the most universal, controversial, enjoyable, irrepressible, ever-continuing human practices. A practice that is the basis and reason for strong emotions, such as love and hate. Empires have risen and fallen, wars have been fought and won and lost, personal fortunes have been affected in many ways, by sexual desircs and sexual rejections. Sexual desire is the second most compelling force in the animal world, which includes man. Without it there would be no families, no children, no continuity of life. The will to live is the strongest force. Our senses must be directed and controlled by the mind. To do this, the mind must have knowledge of the senses and all that they can do. The senses react automatically to the minds command. That is why we have suggested that you practice having your mind consciously trained and your senses to become keener and more aware of their functions. We live in a sex saturated society-that is a problem. Our instincts and interest are easily inflamed and misdirected by a culture that cares little for Bible standards of decency and virtue. Alluring sights and sounds are more omnipresence today than ever, but even the era of photos, computers, and mass media we cannot deny the appearance or appeal of a sexually charged scene, for then we must either be neutered or go out of the world. Rather, the lingering look that turns to craving for what does not belong to us. This is Lust. The Bible confirms that sexual desire and passion are normal human traits. Between man and his wife God affirms and blesses the full-bodied expression of love (-Genesis 2: 24-25) using poetic language, The Bible book of proverbs(Proverbs 5.15-19) describes the joy that can result from appropriate sexual intimacies between husband and wife: "Drink water out of you own cistern and trickling out of the mist of your own well and let your water source proved to be blessed and rejoice with the wife of your youth", a lovable hind an a charming mountain goat. "Let her breasts intoxicate you at all times, with her love may you be in a ecstasy constantly" (proverbs 5: 15, 18, 19) Sexual relations between husband and wife are a God given gift but procreation is not their sole purpose. Sexual relations also allow a married couple to express tenderness and affection for each other. Even beyond matrimony, thoughts with sexual components are not necessarily sinful thoughts-Since Jesus was tempted in all points; He must have experienced His own sexuality as a sinful lust. Thus admiration, appreciation and attraction towards a person of the opposite sex is natural in the human family and may be free of evil intent. Though the interest we feel in people of the opposite gender may be innocent enough, too often we cross that border into the land of lust, as Jesus defined it. Temptation, then has given way to sin, the key victory is preparation before the test. In this corrupt world, how can we prepare ourselves to see no evil? A severe analogy that our Lord used can teach us more. Jesus urges us to ward off lust before it strikes. If your right eye causes you to sin, pluck it out and cast it away from you; for it is more profitable for you that one of your members perish, than for your whole body to be cast into hell (Matthew 5: 29) Do ladies lust? Many admit that they too are tempted by sexy men. Recent statistics suggest that a third of visitors to adult websites are women and that one out of every six women exposed themselves in a way that attracts the improper attention of man. Jesus standard in (Matthew 5: 28) has this corollary for ladies: whoever presents herself with the intent of inciting a man's lust has committed adultery with him already in her heart. No bodily sensation is quite so intensely pleasurable or all consuming as sexual arousal and release. If we regard ourselves merely as bodies and if we therefore want more than anything else to find some way to feel physically good, then sex is the ticket. Men who are tormented with doubts about personal adequacy that rob them of peace and self respect can quickly find a hassle free substitute for masculine fulfillment through sex. Scores of men handle their wive's rejection by having an affair or purchasing a pornography magazine or masturbate while watching an x-rated movie of their fantasy. It works for a short time as they feel really good.

MONEY AND FAME

Money is a protection says the Bible (Ecclesiasts 7: 12) because it pays for food, clothing, and shelter. Money serves as a protection against the hardships associated with poverty. Indeed, in a material way, money can buy practically anything. It meets a response in all things says (Ecclesiastes 10: 19) Money of course become the object of our attention rather than merely a means to get things done. We become susceptible to all sort of immoral temptations including lying, theft, and treachery. Judas Iscariot, one of of Christs apostles betrayed his master for just 30 pieces of silver.An abundance of riches tends to faster self reliance since money appears to grant us a measure of freedom and independence for those who have it a spiritual demise. No wonder the human identity is no longer defined by what one does but by what one owns and our human weakness in this regard is often exploited because if our wants are insatiable, there is simply no such thing as enough. The Bible put it this way in (Ecclesiastes 5 : 10) A mere lover of silver will not be satisfied with silver, neither any lover of wealth with income. That is why a Bible based education can transform our whole mental outlook regarding material things. Spiritual values highlights long-range rewards not short-term gratification Paul wrote: "The things seen materials are temporary, but the things unseen spiritual are everlasting". (2 Corinthians 4: 18) It is true that material pursuits may gratify momentary desires, but greed has no future. Spiritual values are eternal (Proverbs 11: 4 / 1 Corinthians 6: 9-10) Admittedly, to a certain extent, money may serve as a protection but the Bible realistically states: Your money can be gone in a flash, as if it had grown wings and flown away like an eagle (Proverbs 23:5) People have sacrificed a great deal on the alter of materialism, health, families even a good conscience with disastrous results. On the other hand, having spirituality satisfies our most important needs-the need for love, the need for purpose and the need to worship the loving God. There are values that transcend money, prominence, and material wealth. Centuries ago, King Solomon accumulated all that the world could offer in a material way. He built houses and had gardens, orchards, servants, livestock, male and female singers, along with much gold and silver.

Solomon increased his assets far beyond those of all who had preceded him. To say that he was rich is an understatement. Solomon had virtually everything that could be desired yet, when he looked at his accomplishments he said, everything was vanity and a striving under the wind (Ecclesia2:1-11) With the superior wisdom that he was privileged to gain, Solomon knew that greater fulfillment cames from the pursuit of spiritual values. He wrote: The conclusion of the matter, everything having been heard is Fear the true God and keep his commandments.For this is the whole obligation of man (Ecclesiastes 12:13) Along this line we cannot infer that honestly acquired wealth is not inherently good if the owner acknowledged that such wealth is a blessing from God and knows how to handle and use such properly. Such was the case of Abraham, who, during his lifetime, was a wealthy man-Abrahams life proves that it is possible for a man to have great wealth and still be in a right relationship with God. There was a story of this young man who said to God: Two things I ask of you, Oh God do not refuse me before I die: Keep falsehood and lies far from me; give me only my daily bread otherwise I may have too much and say who is God, or I may dishonor the name of my God (Proverbs 30: 7-9) Money is not bad, what is bad is love for money. For the love of money is the root of all kinds of evil. Some people eager for money, have wandered from the faith and pierced themselves with many griefs (1 Timothy 6: 10) The glitter of riches is alluring to mankind. For many, the seemingly natural desire to get rich is a lifelong ambition. So powerful is the desire to have an abundance of these worldly goods that even erstwhile decent men are tempted to set aside time and honored values in exchange for material gain. It is quite easy to understand why people covet to be rich. You see the common belief is that the acquision of wealth leads to a good life, honour and respect. And to many it has even led to power.It is no wonder that even supposedly righteous personalities for example: Ministers of the Evangel also fell prey to the lure of material things. In the words of God, this leads to bareness of life. But the worries of this life, the deceitfulness of wealth and the desire for other things come in and choke the word, making it unfaithful (Mark 4: 19). From infancy man is by nature motivated by self-gratification. Nothing is more important to carnal man than personal interest. Furthermore, man's insatiable avarice for material things knows no end. May it be personal or national interest, the struggle for material competition is undoubtedly man's prime preoccupation. And, this trend has drawn man's consciousness away from the quiet, peaceful and simple living originally designed by the creator of mankind. No amount of cover-up can alter the fact that mankind has plunged downward into the quagmire of materialism. And the sad thing is, it happened not by chance but by choice. This is because materialism is hatched and nurtured in man's heart and mind, thus affecting the very center of the intellect and emotion. In USA and Europe, half of all the marriages of about 60 percent end up in divorces, causing untold heartache and pains. Is there ideal peace in America and Europe? Look at the shocking statistics of crime rate and violence. Even the well-funded CIA and FBI failed to prevent the World Trade Center tragedy.Evidently, wealth is not the answer to life's problems. Everywhere there are people whose wealth has caused more harm than good to their families.Yes, money is not everything in this life. Depending on how it is used, wealth becomes either a boon or a bane to whoever has it. Indeed, Solomon got everything he craved for: wealth, fame, power, wisdom and a harem of 1000 women. What a magnificent example of materialism. One thing often overlooked by man is that riches are fleeting. Yes, it is ephemeral. We learn from King Solomon that riches do not endure forever (Proverbs 27: 24). Now the questions are: where have all the riches of King Solomon gone? Was he able to take his material possessions with him beyond the grave? Let us turn to (1 Timothy 6: 7) for the answer. "For we brought nothing in this world and it is certain that we can carry nothing out of this world" After looking back at his past, the wise king confessed: ″Then I looked on all the works that my hands had worked and on the labour that I had labored to do, and behold, all is vanity and striving after the wind and there was no profit under the sun″ (Ecclesiastes 2:11) Some parents deprived themselves of life's necessities in order to store material possessions for their offsprings. Most people think of wealth as synonymous with happiness. If that were true, then how come some people wallowing in wealth commit suicide or turn recluse? I still remember that famous Hollywood actress who gulped down a bottle of sleeping pills and never woke up, or the American billionaire who turned recluse, preferring to live in seclusion. In either cases, it proves wealth cannot buy true lasting happiness, neither can wealth buy good health or genuine peace. To date, the United States boasts of having the biggest economy and being the wealthiest nation on Earth. Despite Medicare, various diseases claim 2 million American lives each year, with half the deaths being caused by heart related diseases. Many people are living for money and for what it can buy. Some people live to make a name in this world. Others live to perfect their artistic skills. There are also those who live to help others. But many do not know what they are living for or why they are here? Jesus did not live to pursue pleasure. He had his priorities straight. Jesus says: ″Even when a person has an abundance of material things, his life does not result or consist in the abundance of his possessions″. ″He then went on to relate an illustration about a certain rich man who had a crops and who reasoned to himself: what shall I do, now that I have enough crops? I will build bigger storage to store all my crops that I have havested for many years. What was wrong with this man's thinking? The illustration continues: God said to the rich man, unreasonable one, this night i will take away your soul from you. Who then is to have the things you stored up? Even if the man stored his crops, when he died, he could not enjoy the riches he accumulated. In conclusion, Jesus gave this lesson to his audience "So it goes with the man that lays up treasures for himself but is not rich towards God" (Luke 12: 13-21) Yes, we do need some money and enjoyment has its place. However, neither money nor pleasure are the most important thing in life. To be rich toward God, that is to live a life that results in divine favour, is by far the most important thing to pursue. Many people live to make a name for themselves. The desire to make a name, wanting to be remembered by others, is not necessarily bad "A good reputation is better than silver and gold" says the Bible and the day of death than the day of birth (Ecclesiastes 7: 1) On the day of death, the record of the entire life of a man has been written, so to speak. If he has accomplished positive things, the day of that person's death is far better than the day of his birth when the record was totally blank." The writer of the Bible book of Ecclesiastes was King Solomon older half brother. Absalom wanted to make a name for himself". However, his three sons, through whom he could have passed his name on to later generations apparently died young.So what did Absalom do? The scriptures states : Absalom proceeded to raise up for himself a pillar, which is in the low plain of the king, for he said I have no son in order to keep my name in remembrance, so he called the pillar by his own name "(2 Samuel 14:27 ; 18 ; 18) The remains of this pillar have not been found. As for Absalom, he is known to students of the Bible as a notorious rebel who conspired to usurp throne of his father, David. Many today try to be remembered through what they accomplished. They seek glory and fame in the eyes of people whose tastes fluctuate with each passing season.Yet,what happens to such fame? In whose eyes, then should we gain a good reputation? Speaking of certain ones who kept his law, God said through his prophet Isaiah; I will even give to them in my house and within my walls a monument and a name. A name to time indefinite I shall give them, one that will not be cut off (Isaiah 56: 4,5) because of their obedience to God, those acceptable to him will have a monument and a name" God will remember their name to time indefinite, so that they will not be cut off. That is the kind of name the Bible encourages us to have, a fine reputation in the eyes of God. The record of his conduct shows that bones are not all we leave behind when we die. By our actions, we establish a lasting reputation with God, either for good or for evil.

DIVINE LAWS
(The Ten Commandments-Deut 5)

(5) And Moses called all Israel, and said unto them, Hear, O Israel, the statutes and judgments which I speak in your ears this day, that ye may learn them, and keep, and do them. (2)The Lord our God made a covenant with us in Horeb. (3)The Lord made not this covenant with our fathers, but with us, even us, who are all of us here alive this day. (4)The Lord talked with you face to face in the mount out of the midst of the fire, (5) (I stood between the Lord and you at that time, to shew you the word of the Lord: for ye were afraid by reason of the fire, and went not up into the mount;) saying,

(6) I am the Lord thy God, which brought thee out of the land of Egypt, from the house of bondage. (7) Thou shalt have none other gods before me. (8) Thou shalt not make thee any graven image, or any likeness of any thing that is in heaven above, or that is in the earth beneath, or that is in the waters beneath the earth: (9)Thou shalt not bow down thyself unto them, nor serve them: for I the Lord thy God am a jealous God, visiting the iniquity of the fathers upon the children unto the third and fourth generation of them that hate me, (10)And shewing mercy unto thousands of them that love me and keep my commandments. (11) Thou shalt not take the name of the Lord thy God in vain: for the Lord will not hold him guiltless that taketh his name in vain.(12)Keep the sabbath day to sanctify it, as the Lord thy God hath commanded thee.(13)Six days thou shalt labour, and do all thy work: (14)But the seventh day is the sabbath of the Lord thy God: in it thou shalt not do any work, thou, nor thy son, nor thy daughter, nor thy manservant, nor thy maidservant, nor thine ox, nor thine ass, nor any of thy cattle, nor thy stranger that is within thy gates; that thy manservant and thy maidservant may rest as well as thou.(15)And remember that thou wast a servant in the land of

Egypt, and that the Lord thy God brought thee out thence through a mighty hand and by a stretched out arm: therefore the Lord thy God commanded thee to keep the sabbath day.(16) Honour thy father and thy mother, as the Lord thy God hath commanded thee; that thy days may be prolonged, and that it may go well with thee, in the land which the Lord thy God giveth thee.

(17)Thou shalt not kill. (18) Neither shalt thou commit adultery. (19) Neither shalt thou steal. (20)Neither shalt thou bear false witness against thy neighbour. (21)Neither shalt thou desire thy neighbour'swife, neither shalt thou covet thy neighbour's house, his field, or his manservant, or his maidservant, his ox, or his ass, or any thing that is thy neighbour's.

The People's Fear

(22) These words the Lord spake unto all your assembly in the mount out of the midst of the fire, of the cloud, and of the thick darkness, with a great voice: and he added no more. And he wrote them in two tables of stone, and delivered them unto me.(23) And it came to pass, when ye heard the voice out of the midst of the darkness, (for the mountain did burn with fire,) that ye came near unto me, even all the heads of your tribes, and your elders; (24) And ye said, Behold, the Lord our God hath shewed us his glory and his greatness, and we have heard his voice out of the midst of the fire: we have seen this day that God doth talk with man, and he liveth. (25) Now therefore why should we die? for this great fire will consume us: if we hear the voice of the Lord our God any more, then we shall die. (26)For who is there of all flesh, that hath heard the voice of the living God speaking out of the midst of the fire, as we have, and lived? (27)Go thou near, and hear all that the Lord our God shall say: and speak thou unto us all that the Lord our God shall speak unto thee; and we will hear it, and do it. (28)And the Lord heard the voice of your words, when ye spake unto me; and the Lord said

unto me, I have heard the voice of the words of this people, which they have spoken unto thee: they have well said all that they have spoken. (29) that there were such an heart in them, that they would fear me, and keep all my commandments always, that it might be well with them, and with their children for ever! 30)Go say to them, Get you into your tents again. (31) But as for thee, stand thou here by me, and I will speak unto thee all the commandments, and the statutes, and the judgments, which thou shalt teach them, that they may do them in the land which I give them to possess it. (32) Ye shall observe to do therefore as the Lord your God hath commanded you: ye shall not turn aside to the right hand or to the left. (33) Ye shall walk in all the ways which the Lord your God hath commanded you, that ye may live, and that it may be well with you, and that ye may prolong your days in the land which ye shall possess.

The Beginning of the Sermon on the Mount (Matthew 5)

(5)And seeing the multitudes, he went up into a mountain: and when he was set, his disciples came unto him: (2)And he opened his mouth, and taught them, saying,

The Beatitudes

(3) Blessed are the poor in spirit: for theirs is the kingdom of heaven.(4) Blessed are they that mourn: for they shall be comforted. (5) Blessed are the meek: for they shall inherit the earth. (6) Blessed are they which do hunger and thirst after righteousness: for they shall be filled. (7) Blessed are the merciful: for they shall obtain mercy. (8) Blessed are the pure in heart: for they shall see God. (9) Blessed are the peacemakers: for they shall be called the children of God. (10) Blessed are they which are persecuted for righteousness' sake: for theirs is the kingdom of heaven. (11) Blessed are ye, when men shall

revile you, and persecute you, and shall say all manner of evil against you falsely, for my sake.(12)Rejoice, and be exceeding glad: for great is your reward in heaven: for so persecuted they the prophets which were before you.

The Salt of the Earth

13 Ye are the salt of the earth: but if the salt have lost his savour, wherewith shall it be salted? it is thenceforth good for nothing, but to be cast out, and to be trodden under foot of men.

The Light of the World

14 Ye are the light of the world. A city that is set on an hill
cannot be hid.15 Neither do men light a candle, and put it
under a bushel, [2] but on a candlestick; and it giveth light
unto all that are in the house.16 Let your light so shine
before men, that they may see your good works, and glorify your Father which is in heaven.

Jesus' Attitude toward the Law

17 Think not that I am come to destroy the law, or the
prophets: I am not come to destroy, but to fulfil.18 For
verily I say unto you, Till heaven and earth pass, one jot or one tittle shall in no wise pass from the law, till all be
fulfilled. 19 Whosoever therefore shall break one of these least commandments, and shall teach men so, he shall be called the least in the kingdom of heaven: but whosoever shall do and teach them, the same shall be called great in
the kingdom of heaven.20 For I say unto you, That except your righteousness shall exceed the righteousness of the scribes and Pharisees, ye shall in no case enter into the kingdom of heaven.

Jesus' Attitude toward Anger

21 Ye have heard that it was said by them of old time, Thou shalt not kill; and whosoever shall kill shall be in danger of the judgment:22 But I say unto you, That whosoever is angry with his brother without a cause shall be in danger of the judgment:and whosoever shall say to his brother, Raca, [3] shall be in danger of the council: but whosoever shall say, Thou fool, shall be in danger of hell fire.23 Therefore if thou bring thy gift to the altar, and there rememberest that thy brother hath ought against thee;24 Leave there thy gift before the altar, and go thy way; first be reconciled to thy brother, and then come and offer thy gift.25 Agree with thine adversary quickly, whiles thou art in the way with him; lest at any time the adversary deliver thee to the judge, and the judge deliver thee to the officer, and thou be cast into prison.26 Verily I say unto thee, Thou shalt by no means come out thence, till thou hast paid the uttermost farthing.

Jesus' Attitude toward Adultery

27 Ye have heard that it was said by them of old time, Thou shalt not commit adultery:28 But I say unto you, That whosoever looketh on a woman to lust after her hath committed adultery with her already in his heart.29 And if thy right eye offend [4] thee, pluck it out, and cast it from thee: for it is profitable for thee that one of thy members should perish, and not that thy whole body should be cast into hell.30 And if thy right hand offend thee, cut it off, and cast it from thee: for it is profitable for thee that one of thy members should perish, and not that thy whole body should be cast into hell.

Jesus' Attitude toward Divorce

31 It hath been said, Whosoever shall put away his wife, let him give her a writing of divorcement:32 But I say unto

you, That whosoever shall put away his wife, saving for the cause of fornication, causeth her to commit adultery: And whosoever shall marry her that is divorced committeth adultery.

Jesus' Attitude toward Oaths

33 Again, ye have heard that it hath been said by them of
old time, Thou shalt not forswear thyself, but shalt perform
unto the Lord thine oaths:34 But I say unto you, Swear not
at all; neither by heaven; for it is God's throne:35 Nor by
the earth; for it is his footstool: neither by Jerusalem; for it
is the city of the great King.36 Neither shalt thou swear by
thy head, because thou canst not make one hair white or
black.37 But let your communication be, Yea, yea; Nay,
nay: for whatsoever is more than these cometh of evil.

Love for Enemies

38 Ye have heard that it hath been said, An eye for an eye,
and a tooth for a tooth:39 But I say unto you, That ye resist
not evil: but whosoever shall smite thee on thy right cheek,
turn to him the other also.40 And if any man will sue thee
at the law, and take away thy coat, let him have thy cloke
also.41 And whosoever shall compel thee to go a mile, go
with him twain.42 Give to him that asketh thee, and from
him that would borrow of thee turn not thou away.

43 Ye have heard that it hath been said, Thou shalt love
thy neighbour, and hate thine enemy.44 But I say unto
you, Love your enemies, bless them that curse you, do
good to them that hate you, and pray for them which
despitefully use you, and persecute you;45 That ye may be
the children of your Father which is in heaven: for he
maketh his sun to rise on the evil and on the good, and
sendeth rain on the just and on the unjust.46 For if ye love
them which love you, what reward have ye? do not even
the publicans the same?47 And if ye salute your brethren
only, what do ye more than others? do not even the

publicans so?48 Be ye therefore perfect, even as your Father which is in heaven is perfect.

THE GOLDEN RULE

(Mt 7:12)

1. We come now to **verse 12**, where we find the **"GOLDEN RULE"**...

2. This "rule" serves as a perfect summary of the kind of righteousness the kingdom of heaven expects in respect to man's relation to man.
But what is the "golden rule"? Was Jesus teaching anything new or original by what He stated? Well, in a way it was something new.

I. THE "GOLDEN RULE" VERSUS THE "SILVER RULES"

A. Many people believe Jesus was simply repeating what others had already taught; for example.

1. The HINDU religion taught:

This is the sum of duty: do naught to others which if done to thee would cause thee pain.

The Mahabharata

2. The BUDDHIST religion taught:

Hurt not others with that which pains yourself.

Udana-Varga

3. The JEWISH traditions taught:

What is hateful to you, do not to your fellow men. That is the entire Law; all the rest is commentary.

The Talmud

4. The MUSLIM religion taught:

No one of you is a believer until he desires for his brother that which he desires for himself.

Hadith

5. The BAHA'I faith teaches:

He should not wish for others that which he doth not wish for himself, nor promise that which he doth not fulfil.

The Book of Certitude

6. And Yet Some Other Sources:

Do not do unto others what angers you if done to you by others.

Isocrates 436-338 BCE

"Tzu-kung asked, 'Is there a single word which can be a guide to conduct throughout one's life?' The Master said, 'It is perhaps the word "shu". Do not impose on others what you yourself do not desire'"

Analects, 15.24

B. BUT JESUS' "RULE" WAS POSITIVE

1. Jesus' "rule" requires you to do something favorably to others,while the others only prohibit you from doing

something unfavorably to others!

a. **Jesus** -Do unto others what you want them to do to you

b.**Others** -Don't do to others what you don't want done to you

2. With the others, all that is required is that you don't harm other people; with Jesus, what is required is that you show kindness to others

3. Jesus' rule is truly the GOLDEN rule, the others are SILVER
rules (of value, yes, but not as much as "gold")

[The only exception appears to be that found in Hadith (the traditions of Islam); but then, some of Islam is admittedly based upon what Jesus taught 600 years before Mohammed.

So what Jesus taught was something new compared to what "uninspired"Teachers had taught prior.

But in another sense it was nothing new; rather, in a simple and easy to remember statement, Jesus gives us.

II. A GUIDELINE FOR RIGHTEOUS CONDUCT TOWARDS OTHERS

A. That was in perfect harmony with the law and the prophets.!

1. Just as we have seen in the rest of Jesus' teachings (cf.Matthew 5:21-48

2. This one "rule" summarizes what the Law and the Prophets were
all about.

3. Just as the commandment **"Love your neighbor as**

yourself" summed up the Law according to Paul – Roman 13: 8-10

B. A SORT OF "POCKET KNIFE" OR "CARPENTER'S RULE"...

1. That is, something that is always ready to be used

2. For example, even in an emergency, when there is no time to consult a friend, teacher, or book for advice, the "golden rule" can be guide for proper conduct.

3. Treat others as you would be treated, and it is unlikely you will ever do the wrong thing.

1. Even in this way, we find that Jesus did not come to "destroy" the Law, but to fulfill it in every way, including summarizing its righteousness in ways easy for us to understand and apply!

2. Throughout the first **twelve verses** of Matthew 7, then, there is a continuous theme: the righteousness of the kingdom in regards to man's dealings with man.

NECESSITY KNOWS NO LAW

Survival, Sex, Stomach. These are the strongest emotions known to all creatures on this Earth. They are the reason for practically every actions that is put in motion. Can you give a hungry man some food to share to his neighbours without him eating some part or portion of the food? The answer is emphatically no.

This issue are worldwide and unquestionable to all nations and to nearly everyone who has walked on this Earth or lived in this Gods Great School For Mankind we commonly call Earth.

Be it in Europe, Asia, Australia, Africa or America, the fact remains the same. Biblical and secular history contain many examples of people who stole, perverted justice, prostituted themselves, committed murder, betrayed others, and lied – all for money.

Consider the following examples:

On one occasion, David sought refuge with Achish, King of the Philistine city of Gath, the home of Goliath (1 Samuel 21: 10-15)The Kings servants denounced David as an enemy of their nation. How did David react in that dangerous situation?

He poured out his spirit in prayer to God (Psalm56:1-4,11-13)Although he had to feign insanity to get away, David knew that it was God who had delivered him by blessing his efforts.(Psalm 34:4-6,9-11)This does not mean that we simply hand our problems over to God without doing what we can about them and expect God to act in our behalf. David did not pray to

God for help and then leave the matters like that .He used the physical and intellectual ability that God granted him to tackled the problem at hand, yet David knew that human efforts alone could not be counted for success.On another occasion, Jesus healed on the Sabbath Day, and it was against the Jewish law to work or do such a thing as Jesus did. But Jesus had to do what He did to save the life of that patient and that is where necessity knows no law comes in again.

The third example is : If there is a fire outbreak or an ambulance carrying an ill person is urgently rushing to hospital , when reaching the traffic light and it happens that the light is on red, would the firefighter or the ambulance driver obey the traffic light and stop just because the driver does not want to disrespect the traffic light? The correct answer is no without second thought .

Undoubtedly, necessity can prompt attitude and actions capable of compelling someone to act rightly or wrongly depending on the circumstances that one may find himself or herself in.

FLAWED WORKFORCE

What sort of person does God use?

Imagine a group of people gathered before you. It is your job to select from among them those mostly to play a pivotal role in Gods plan for humanity.

Because these people know you well and are at ease, they open up and share their darkest secrets. One tells you that after a night of heavy drinking, he was sexually abused by one of his own children.

Another confesses that he gave his wife for another man to sleep with. Yet another plotted to kill the husband of his mistress. Another murdered a man and still on the run from justice. One is a prostitute. Another has a lifestyle marked by violence; he even killed people to impress a girlfriend and his prospective father in-law. Yet another confesses that he cheated his brother out of his inheritance.

Now, who is a saint and who is spotless? No one is incapable of sin or mistake and there is no age limit in committing sin or making mistakes thus, no man or woman is free from this trait. The Biblical Noah became drunk and was sexually abused.

Abraham gave his wife to sleep with another man. David plotted to have his husband killed. Moses murdered an Egyptian and was never brought to account. Rahab was the prostitute, and Samson killed to impress to his girlfriend. Jacob cheated to get his brother's inheritance and blessing.Yes, God uses flawed people who are, in the eyes of man, imperfect resources. We often expect that a person of a great faith and good service will be relatively untouched by sin. This example from the Bible shows us that faithful people are also flawed people. They are resilient folks who have recovered from acts of evil and disobedience to perform great acts of loyalty and faith. Chances are that you have a checkered past and are telling yourself that you have made too many mistakes for God to use you. Bear in mind, however, that it is not about you but about what God can do through you, if you let Him. He is far more patient and forgiving that we. God does not tolerate a refusal to stop sinning, but gives grace to the humble and gladly uscs a heart that has been broken for him.

DO YOU MEASURE YOURSELF WITH OTHERS

Do you measure yourself against others? Who of us has not met a person who is better looking than we are, seems to be more popular, grasps things faster, or gets better grades in school? Maybe others have better health or a more gratifying job, are more successful, or seem to have more friends. They may have more possessions, more money, a newer car, or they may just seem to be happier. In noting such things, do we measure ourselves against others? Are comparisons inevitable?

One concept of why people may compare themselves with others is that this serves to maintain or enhance their self-esteem. People are often satisfied to find that they are as successful as their peers. Another idea is that comparisons are attempts to reduce uncertainty about ourselves, to understand what we are capable of doing and what our limits are. We observe what others have achieved. If they are like us in many respects and have reached certain objectives, we might feel that we can reach similar goals. Comparisons are most often made between people who resemble one another, who are of the same sex and of a similar age if not the same and at a similar social level and who know one another .We are less likely to measure ourselves against someone else if the perceived disparity is great. Put another way, the average teenager girl is less likely to compare herself with a top model than with her school mates, and the model is unlikely to compare herself with the teenager.In what area do comparisons take place? Any possession or attribute considered of value in a community be it intelligence, beauty, wealth, clothes-may be the basis for comparison. However, we tend to draw comparisons with things that interest us.We will probably not envy the size of the stamp collection of one of our acquaintances, for example, unless we are particularly interested in collecting stamps.

Comparisons elicit a whole spectrum of reactions, ranging from contentment to depression, from admiration and a desire for emulation to uneasiness or antagonism. Regarding competitive comparisons, many who strive to come off winners in comparisons display a competitive spirit.They want to be better than others, and they are not content until they feel that they are.

Our failures are all the more painful when it seems that people who are in the same situation as we are have procured the possessions that we want. A competitive spirit thus provokes envy, resentment, and displeasure toward someone because of his belongings, property, possessions, position, reputation, advantages, and so on. This leads to more competition- a vicious circle by degrading the achievements of rivals, envious ones attempt to save their own injured-self esteem. Such reactions may seem petty, but if not recognized and checked, they can lead to malicious wrongdoing .

Consider the two Bible accounts in which necessity and envy was a twin factor .During his residence among the Philistines, Isaac was blessed with flocks of sheeps and herds of cattle and a large body of servants so that the Philistines began to envy him. They reacted by stopping up the wells dug by Isaac's father, Abraham, and their king asked Isaac to leave the area.(Gen 26:1-3,12-16) Their envy was spiteful and destructive .They just could not bear Isaac's enjoyment of prosperity in their midst any longer.Centuries later, David distinguished himself on the battlefield His feats were celebrated by the women of Israel, who sang: Saul has struck down his thousands, and David his tens of thousands. Though he was receiving a measure of praise, Saul considered that comparison to be demeaning and envy stirred in his heart. From then on, he nurtured ill will toward David. He soon made the first of several attempts to kill David. What wicked can spring from necessity so if measuring ourselves against others- their feats or advantages stimulates feelings akin to necessity, envy and competitiveness. These are negative emotions incompatible with God's thinking .God do not create all equal, that’s why we have different abilities depending on a variety of factors. There will always be some who seem be doing better that we are. Hence, rather than observing them enviously, we should gauge our performance in relationship to God's righteous standards.

A WORLDWIDE MORAL BREAKDOWN

Uganda works for large trading company in London, while visiting thc factory of a potential supplier , he expressed concern about whether the factory could meet the standards needed to produce his company's products. Later, at dinner, the factory manager gave Uganda an envelope .Inside, Uganda's found a bribe amounting to tens of thousands of dollars in cash- the equivalent of his annual salary.

Uganda's experience is far from unique . Around the world, the scope and pervasiveness of dishonesty is staggering. For example, court documents show that between 2001 and 2007, a large German industrial firm paid 1.4 billion dollars in bribes to obtain contracts.

Although recent high profile corporate scandals have led to some reforms, the overall situation appears to be worsening. A 2010 study by Transparency International found that worldwide levels of corruption have increased in the previous three years.

Hurricane Katarina which hit the United States late in 2005 produced one of the most extraordinary displays of scams, schemes and stupefying bureaucratic bungles in modern history.

In many countries, it is customary for business transactions to be accompanied by an exchange of gifts. Depending on the size and circumstances of the gifts, the boundaries of honest business practices can easily become blurred. In many lands, corrupt officials demand money before performing their duties and willingly accept payment in exchange for special treatment.

A fifty year old woman in Queensland, Australia began online romance with a man she thought was a British engineer. She had paid out 47.000 australian dollar before it was discovered that he was a twenty-seven year old conman in Nigeria.

Many fraudulent contacts on the internet takes place through email. The kind of email that this woman received is called phishing email. Like baiting fish, such email coaxes the recipient to supply her password, credit card numbers or bank accounts informations to an authentic looking but fake website. Beware of emails that contain suspicious links .Sometimes, a Trojan Horse , or Trojan can provide backdoor access to your computer system , which may allow scammers to have access to your private information.

Phishing: email that coaxes the recipient to supply his password, credit card numbers, or bank account information to an authentic looking but fake website.

Spy software: A programme that records your computer activity.

Trojan Horse: A programme designed to breach the security of a computer system while seemingly performing some harmless function.

Perhaps you have received online messages stating: Your computer is at risk, click here to protect your computer, or free screen savers. Click here. If you click there, you could activate spy software. Also, if you are looking for a job on the internet, beware; scammers use phony online sites to collect registration fees and even personal financial data.

Thieves are now smarts enough to access remotely the databases of companies or financial institutions and steal data. In May 2007, criminals hacked the computer system of a department store chain in the United States and gained access to millions of customers records, including credit card informations.

In Nigeria, criminals got into the databases of several banks and stole 1.8 million personal identification numbers to withdraw money from automated teller machines.

There is now a thriving online black market where rogue employees and hackers sell stolen credit card data and even peoples full identities.

UNLOCK YOUR LATENT POTENTIALS

It would be unreal not to recognize that there is a physical side of our being .Most of the day-to-day pleasures that we enjoy and many of the pains we suffer exist in this house, in this material being (ie) our body. To say that earthly , bodily pleasures are unimportant would be ridiculous and unacceptable. Most of the functions that are necessary to create, maintain and sustain life are actually physically enjoyable: eating, the sex act, are examples, and all give pleasure and even ecstasy. But in an effort and struggles to survive and to make the ends meet, that would not be reasons for committing crimes or doing evil things such as robbing others or doing something against someone's will.You should always remember to respect and comply with the Golden Rule: Do unto others as you would like them to do to you .

Everyone has talent or some talents but it is up to you to discover where your latent or untapped talent lies, develop it and put it into use for the benefit of yourself and others.

This reminds me the Bible story where Jesus shared some talents to two people and the first person put his own into use while the other person hid his own under the Earth. When Jesus returned to ask them how well they used their talents, the first person produced a positive result with his own talents and even multiplied it and it became many while the other person did not have anything to show for it , because he was lazy and thought that the world owed him a living. The Book of Bible put it this way:

15 To one he gave five talents, to another two, and to
another one, each according to his ability. Then he went on
his journey. **16** The one who had received five talents went
off right away and put his money to work and gained five

more. **17** In the same way, the one who had two gained
two more. **18** But the one who had received one talent
went out and dug a hole in the ground and hid his master's
money in it. **19** After a long time, the master of those
slaves came and settled his accounts with them. **20** The
one who had received the five talents came and brought
five more, saying, 'Sir, you entrusted me with five talents.
See, I have gained five more.' **21** His master answered,
'Well done, good and faithful slave! You have been
faithful in a few things. I will put you in charge of many
things. Enter into the joy of your master.' **22** The one with
the two talents also came and said, 'Sir, you entrusted two
talents to me. See, I have gained two more.' **23** His master
answered, 'Well done, good and faithful slave! You have
been faithful with a few things. I will put you in charge of
many things. Enter into the joy of your master.'

24 Then the one who had received the one talent came
and said, 'Sir, I knew that you were a hard man, harvesting
where you did not sow, and gathering where you did not
scatter seed,

25 so I was afraid, and I went and hid your talent in the
ground. See, you have what is yours.' **26** But his master
answered, 'Evil and lazy slave! So you knew that I harvest
where I didn't sow and gather where I didn't scatter? **27**
Then you should have deposited my money with the
bankers, and on my return I would have received my
money back with interest! **28** Therefore take the talent
from him and give it to the one who has ten. **29** For the
one who has will be given more, and he will have more
than enough. But the one who does not have, even what he
has will be taken from him. **30** And throw that worthless
slave into the outer darkness, where there will be weeping
and gnashing of teeth.' So in conclusion, we should ask
ourselves questions like is there anything special or unique
in me as Talent(s) that I can develop to help myself and
others. Clearly, if you acquire all the Wisdoms of King

Solomon without putting them in use .

It will be absoutely useless. Search yourself, and for sure you will find something unique and special in you, that makes you, the You , you are .

THE ERRORS OF OUR FATHERS

Anyone who might have lived a hundred years ago would tell a far different story about the world and life upon it than someone living today. Picture how the difference would be over a period of a thousand years.

It was acceptable a hundred years ago to hold a human being as a slave. A writer, at that time would not be shocked, as we would today, by a man or woman being treated as a chattel and in many instances, like an animal.

On the other hand, if someone, a hundred years ago, would have seriously said that man would fly through space and land on the moon and then back again to Earth , that person would be locked up for being crazy or even burned as a witch, which was all right to do then but hardly possible to do today.

If by some unlikely miracle your great, great grandfather were to return to Earth today, exactly the way he was when he left it sixty or seventy or so years ago and you were to pick him up in your automobile in a woods at the edge of town…how would you explain your auto and ask him to get in?

When you finally got him into the car, you touched the starter and the engine came to life and you drove onto the wide, smooth, concrete highway and zipped off at 55 miles an hour.How would he react? Then you turned on the radio in this moving car and listened to an announcer in a radio station a hundred miles away, calmly described a record that he was about to play a record that had been made thirty years before in a studio several thousand miles away by a singer who had died ten years back, and your car was filled with the music of a thirty-seven piece orchestra accompanying this singer. Do you think grand pa would understand? Time has changed!

The principal errors of our fathers lies in the fact that our fathers brought us into this world without plans. Plans, in the sense that nothing was put aside like money, education applications, social welfare and child upbringing pre-arrangements ,discover what this child could do best and helping and encouraging this child to understand the values of his or her potentials while guiding this child as his mentor in order to make a good choice of career that will suit him in the near future as well as applying the necessary tools to further develop this child's latent potentials so that by so doing this child will have a pattern in life that will inevitably foster and boost his self esteem as well as giving him an edge towards success in this increasingly competitive world. Remember that, if you fail to plan then you have planned to fail and that's how it goes. The same as sowing and reaping or as you make your bed, so you lie on it.

They stubbornly didn't want to open their eyes to see or figure out the errors of their own ancestors or forefathers and adopt a positive attitude to reverse them for the betterment of their own period of existence and that of the forthcoming generations, so to speak. Some fathers used their own tongues to kill their own child simply because they were ignorant of the powers of the spoken words. To speak is to create, because when you speak something for good or for bad it is like where you have just planted a seed and it takes time for this seed to grow because this seed will pass through various stages before it will become matured and produce fruit. Similarly, the same is with the spoken words. When a father got angry because he had been offended and then believed that the only way he would scold his stubborn child was by speaking evil things to his child, the same negative effects will follow that child, knowingly or unknowingly .One of the reasons is because the Father is the physical God's representation on Earth to this child ,just like a visible god to the child. Therefore these are one of the many ways we suffer because of our father's negligence to civilized education and spiritual education as well. Some fathers unwillfully killed their own children .Yes, they killed their children with their tongues by wishing, thinking and pronouncing bad things against their children when they were upset or provoked. Little did they know that they are the ones that brought suffering to their children because they lack civilized and spiritual education, therefore their problem became self-created or self-made and not God made. In my village, where I came from, one day as I went to the market square. I saw a mad man and he walked towards me and asked me for some money to buy some food and I gave him some coins. After returning back from market I met my mother at home and I quickly narrated the story of the lunatic man I saw in the market square to her and she said to me that the lunatic man was one of the sons of our village chief's son. She continued: that he village chief did something wrong to the village people and he was summoned to the village community centre for interrogation. In his explanation, the village chief swore by saying that if what they are accusing him of , is what he did let one of his son become Mad , but if he is not responsible for what they are accusing of, then nothing should happen to his son.

So you can see how the powers of the spoken words and our parents deeds can affect us .I want every father and mother to learn this lesson and reverse their bad words to good words when reading this book and to maintain positive and pure speech whenever they are speaking especially, to their own offsprings and to others too.

The same goes to those of our mothers and fathers who do not realize that their tongues are a small part of human parts but very powerful when set in motion. All these are as a result of ignorance.Ignorance of who we are in the creations of God.We are not ordinary beings but spiritually energized beings, so you should be extremely careful in your choice of words. Infact, ignorance is the root causes of human suffering. Now imagine that you are living in a house where gold is buried underneath and you are looking for someone who could give you some gold so that you can sell it and make some money whereas, there are Big quantities of gold beneath your house. That is a typical example of ignorance .We are not robots that are conditioned to function in a particular expected manner, no, we are humans created in the image and likeness of God. It is the God in us or our conscious that tells us what is good or what is bad. That is the image of God in us and nothing else.

There are three types of educations namely: **worldly education**, **civilized education and spiritual education**. **In worldly education**, you are thought a lesson practically and are given answers without detailed explanations and proven facts to sum it up. Unfortunately this is the type of education that our ancestors, and greatgrand fathers passed on to our present modern fathers but some of our fathers rejected this worldly education because they used their wisdom to discard any teachings that do not conform to moral standards.

Civilized education equipped us with the knowledge of reading, writing, speaking foreign languages, brings us a wealth of insight about our body functions and our health, knowledge about the world in which we live, including how to calculate things enabling us to know our fundamental human rights and the laws under which we are protected and the things which are lawful and unlawful.

Spiritual education takes us to the beginning of this world with creations, the first human couple, God and Jesus, The fall of Satan, moral conducts. Spiritual laws of causes and effects.

Obviously, the Bible is considered the greatest document on Earth and it had stood the test of time right from the time immemorial to this present time and forever and ever.

About the Author of This Book.

A 21ST Century world-class writer, **Shannon S. Keys**, cuts to the heart of Biblical views of Divine principals in respect to life.This unique book conveys useful insights that touches major areas of human life. Undoubtedly, this book of insight must stand the test of time because some of its writings and quotations were extracted from the Holy Bible.

www.ingramcontent.com/pod-product-compliance
Ingram Content Group UK Ltd.
Pitfield, Milton Keynes, MK11 3LW, UK
UKHW040011200726
13854UKWH00001B/151

9 781789 553765